To Bar

love
Mrs Shirley.
x

Extraordinary Shorts

BY MELODY STARKEY

Matador
9 Priory Business Park,
Wistow Road, Kibworth Beauchamp,
Leicestershire. LE8 0RX
Tel: 0116 279 2299
Email: books@troubador.co.uk
Web: www.troubador.co.uk/matador
Twitter: @matadorbooks

ISBN 978 1785892 776

British Library Cataloguing in Publication Data.
A catalogue record for this book is available from the British Library.

Printed and bound in the UK by TJ International, Padstow, Cornwall
Typeset in 11pt Garamond by Troubador Publishing Ltd, Leicester, UK

Matador is an imprint of Troubador Publishing Ltd

*My Mum and Dad, who encouraged my love of
literature and the arts.*

*My husband Alan, daughter Jessicae, family and friends
who supported me throughout this process.*

*Beth Blake my brilliant illustrator
who has made my ideas come to life.*

*Hundreds of children who I have taught and all the teaching staff
who I have had the pleasure of working with.*

Contents

A Cornish Encounter

The crooked steps to the quayside seemed to be more slippery in the fading light. Jamie's battered football dribbled annoyingly right down to the bottom and luckily became tangled in the long grass.

"I told you to keep that under control…" His dad's voice sounded a long way off, but mercifully he didn't seem to be too cross.

Jamie's trainers skidded precariously on the last few stones. He grabbed the offending ball and glanced across Mevagissey Harbour. He loved this place, although sometimes it had been dreadful weather; each holiday held a hundred crowded memories.

A boy of about the same age stared at him from the harbour wall. Piercing, blue eyes; dusky, tanned cheeks and a shock of unruly, blonde hair.

"You playing?" he asked quietly in soft Cornish tones, "you're not local then?"

Jamie shook his head, always shy with new people.

"Where you staying then?"

"Number 33 Polkirk Hill."

"Oh, Gig Cottage! Right, I'll call later."

The ball slipped out of Jamie's hands again, but when he looked up, the boy had gone.

They had takeaway fish and chips that night: gloriously greasy, but so fresh and plump, every mouthful was amazing. Mum and dad settled in front of the TV, exhausted after a day's sightseeing. Jamie kept glancing out of the tiny bottle glass window in the front door of their quaint holiday cottage and wondered if his new acquaintance would call.

It was almost dark; the street lights had begun to glow and were reflected in the pools of rainwater on the narrow pavements – and then the knock came. Jamie opened the door as quietly as he could, as he knew that his parents wouldn't let him out at this time.

"Keep your window open!"

The boy's words were almost inaudible. Again he vanished into the shadows. Jamie pulled the wooden shutters across the salt-smeared windows and shuddered. There was a funny feeling in this little old-fashioned kitchen with its range that bore the words 'Not Working Properly Just Retained For Character'.

He couldn't sleep in his tiny room with the thick, uneven walls. It was very stuffy and so he did leave the squeaky sash window wide open.

It must have been a little after midnight when the first flurry of tiny stones landed with a clatter on the slate floor. He jumped up at once and leaned right out into the cooler night air. The street lights seemed dimmer somehow.

"Well, are you coming or not then?" This time the boy's voice, coming from the street below, was far more lively and insistent. Jamie grabbed his shorts and t-shirt, didn't bother with socks and struggled to squeeze into damp trainers, not forgetting the all-important football.

Almost without thinking, he slid down the rusty

drainpipe and landed awkwardly against the living room window. He held his breath; he really would be in trouble if he was caught, but somehow he couldn't resist the temptation. At the time he didn't notice that the ground seemed much more uneven than in the daytime.

The boy's face appeared from the shadows, his friendly smile putting Jamie at ease.

"Come on, there's a nice grassy bit at the top of this hill!"

Both boys raced over the cobbles and Jamie marvelled at the fact that this Cornish character had bare feet. They played in the moonlight for what seemed like hours, laughing and skidding; not saying much, but enjoying their obvious mutual love of sport.

A pale, pinkish light started to show over the silver sea and Jamie realised he would need to get back to the little cottage, and anyway, how was he going to climb back up? He shared his fears with his friend whose name he still didn't know. Again, too shy to ask.

"Oh, don't worry, I'll give you a bunk up!" the Cornish lad reassured him.

The boys walked together as if they were old friends.

"See you tomorrow?" Jamie asked timidly. No answer, but his companion was true to his word, pushing him up strongly, and he managed to scramble up the drainpipe back into his room, just lit dimly now by the palest of suns. The ball followed him, expertly lobbed from below.

The last he saw of the young Cornish boy was his slight silhouette, sharp against the pale sunrise.

Later that morning, rain literally bounced off the cobblestones near to the cottage wall. While mum and dad were poring over leaflets to decide where to avoid the weather, Jamie decided to see what he could find to play with in the games cupboard. He opened a rather stiff drawer in the old sideboard. Inside was a single sepia photograph dated 1883.

An unmistakeable face grinned back at him. He was clutching a leather football.

A Friend Indeed

The wind howled around the old lighthouse which seemed to sway in response to the rages of the storm. Rain fell in torrents mercilessly and the angry waves rose up out of the dark sea to greet it head on. Paije peered out of her bedroom window and shuddered. What a night! Not one to be travelling about on, especially not near the coast. She loved the sea, even in weather like this; it was so wild and unpredictable — rather like herself, she thought a little sadly. Her father was always saying that he didn't understand her and that she wasn't like 'normal' girls of her age. But what was normal? She didn't want to be the same as everyone else: she liked sailing in his battered old boat, fishing and swimming for miles on hot, sunny days. She didn't have many friends, but that never seemed to matter.

As she drew back from the glass, streaked with rain, she saw the unmistakeable shape of a dog lit up fleetingly by the lighthouse beam as it swung around the beach. The poor creature was racing up and down, probably barking, but drowned out by the noise of the storm. Paije didn't recognise it and got out her binoculars to get a closer look. She could just make out an odd-looking, dark object near the water line. What was it? The dog was circling it now, getting drenched as the waves crept up the shingle. The tide was coming in… all at once Paije realised that the shape was a person, obviously ill or injured. Her stomach gave a lurch; soon the water would cover the entire beach. She had to help.

Mum was away for a few days looking after Gran. Dad was on duty at the lighthouse for another hour yet. Paije hesitated, then picked up the phone to ring him; would he believe her? She was often having imaginary adventures and experiencing emergency situations which amounted to nothing.

"Dad, I think someone's stranded on the beach and the tide is coming in, I don't know what to do!" She tried not to make her voice sound as panicky as she felt. Her dad, tired from his long shift, played the situation down by saying he would phone the coastguard and not to worry. On no account was she to go down to the beach.

Paije was not a disobedient girl, notwithstanding all her failings, but the minutes ticked by and no comforting headlights appeared over the headland. No sign of a coastguard. The storm raged on and the water crept ever near to the body on the cold sand near the water's edge.

She phoned her dad again and he assured her that help was on its way. That was not enough to satisfy Paije. With one more anxious look out of the window, she raced downstairs and dragged on her waterproof jacket. The cat blinked irritably at her from the warmth of the hearth.

It was hard to open the front door; the wind was pushing against it like a giant invisible hand trying to stop her from going out. Eventually, she squeezed through; it slammed shut again and her breath was almost taken away by the awful weather.

The dark trees which lined the crooked path down to the beach bent over her as if to hinder her progress. She swept away their dark branches, her mind intent on just getting there in time.

She slipped precariously on the loose shingle at the top of the beach, falling forward and scraping her knees on a sharp rock. The dog had seen her and bounded over to bark furiously as if in relief. They ran as well as they could side by side; the water was already surrounding the poor soul sprawled out before them.

Paije shook the mound of clothes, staggered to see a girl not much older than herself, obviously unconscious, with a nasty gash on the side of her head.

Paije knew she had to move her and had no time to worry about making her injuries worse. She linked her arms around the top half of the limp body and pulled with all her might. The dog was pulling her coat as if it was the right thing to do.

Somehow they managed to get to the top of the beach and Paije fell, exhausted, her dark hair dripping into her eyes so that she couldn't see more than a metre in front of her. Then mercifully, headlights appeared at the top of the cliff path, and several people could be heard running towards them. Everything was going to be all right. Paije held the girl's head as she started to murmur.

"It's okay, you're safe now."

Paije went to see Karen, for that was the girl's name, every day after that. The hospital was only a short bus ride away. They became the greatest of friends and Karen explained how she had been walking that evening and had tripped, banging her head on a rock.

"Good job your dog was there!" Paije grinned at her new friend, "I would never have noticed you if it hadn't been for him."

"But that's just it," said Karen, struggling up against the starched pillows, "I haven't got a dog!"

Weeks later, when Karen was more or less fully recovered, they came upon a group of little, old stones encircled by a small fence. Each one had a name written on it and a rough carving of a cat or a dog.

"A pet cemetery!" Paije exclaimed, and bent down to get a closer look. One that had a dog on it bore another inscription: 'Blackie — A friend in need is a friend indeed'.

"I wonder," whispered Karen, her blue eyes widening.

"I *know,*" replied Paije with a smile as she touched the stone gently. Somewhere in the distance a dog barked and then all was still.

A Step In Time

"Don't get on the bus, Jonathan Parkins, until I'm there to count you!" Mrs. Spencer strode through the lines of children, waving her clipboard above their heads.

"Now, stand STILL — are you all right, Mrs. Wood?" Mrs. Wood nodded, almost flattened against the railings by the excited pupils. Perhaps, it would have been better to stay at home and do the ironing – still, it got her out of the house, helping with Year 5's 'Victorian Experience' trip. She smiled faintly at Mrs. Spencer who was now perched on the top step, counting everyone onto the bus.

"Right, driver, that's the lot; who's got the sick bucket?"

Jon had raced to the back of the bus, of course, and sat dangling his legs on the long seat. His best friend, Rafee, knelt up beside him, already making rude signs to the Land Rover unfortunate enough to draw up behind them. Trips were always a good excuse to have a good time. Mrs. Spencer inevitably got into a flap and, consequently, her iron grip on the class was somewhat relaxed. Jon giggled at the Land Rover driver's angry face. Rafee threw a piece of chewing gum down the length of the bus and it landed beautifully in Lucy Austin's long, silky hair. Perfect, she had no idea! Jon stuffed a fist into his mouth and pretended to look out of the window.

Ten minutes later they arrived at the Open Victorian Museum. Mrs. Spencer took a deep breath and held up her hand for silence.

"I am still waiting, Rafee Ahmad!" He crawled out from under the seat.

"I lost my pencil, miss!"

Mrs. Spencer frowned but ignored him. She ushered them off the bus, confiscated two iPods, a mobile phone and a bag of Blow Bigga Gum. The bus driver closed the doors — thankfully — and settled back with his newspaper.

"Huh, Victorians, boring!" moaned Jon, glaring at the posters outside.

"No, it's great; lots of potential," whispered Rafee. Everyone trooped into a kind of playground. A smiling lady in full Victorian costume came out, acting 'in role' and showed them to a room where they had to put on the clothes of Victorian children. Jon and Rafee hung back, but couldn't escape permanently. Fully kitted out in knee length trousers, waistcoats and peaked caps, they purposefully made their way to the back of the line.

"I feel like a real wally in this!" moaned Jon, pulling his hat down over his face.

"You look like one too!" retorted Rafee, snatching the offending object from Jon's head and tossing it over his shoulder. They both laughed and ran away from the main group. The wind blew the checked cap further across the playground. Both boys raced after it, elbowing each other in friendly contest.

Neither of them paid much attention to the fog that had begun to swirl about them, each boy intent on getting the hat first. Rafee stretched out, fell, and rolled over on the concrete, laughing uncontrollably.

"Now look what you've done!" smirked Jon, "your trousers are all ripped, you'll be for it!"

Rafee didn't reply; he was looking intently at two grey shapes approaching in the distance. He stared hard; the fog was now so thick, the whole of the old Victorian school building was obscured.

It was two boys.

"Old Crabby's on the warpath!" shouted one, "you'd better come quickly or it's the birch for you!"

Jon and Rafee looked at each other, serious for once. Neither of them recognised the two characters standing near them. Their costumes were very good and they both looked decidedly grubby. One boy had no socks on and a toe poked through the hole in his boot.

"Which school are you from then?" asked Rafee curiously.

"This one, of course; haven't seen you before though," muttered the taller of the two. "Get a move on, if you know what's good for you!" They both ran off.

Jon and Rafee followed in their general direction, the fog still as thick as soup, making them cough and splutter as they went. Eventually, they arrived at the school house and pushed the heavy door tentatively. Not a single sound came from the room that lay before them, despite it being crammed full of rows of pale faced children of all shapes and sizes. They were stood as if to attention with their hands behind their backs. Yet they were not the children from their class; it must be another school visiting.

"Oh, so you have decided to join us, have you?" the teacher's voice bellowed from the far side of the room, making the boys jump and back away.

"Get inside, you miserable specimens. One hundred lines each at playtime!"

"I hope she's acting," whispered Jon, "anyway, I'll tell her we're in the wrong…"

"Silence! Speak when you are asked to and not before!" the teacher roared and slammed an ominous-looking birch rod onto her high desk. She peered at them over her half-moon glasses, the hairs on her chin almost bristling as she spoke.

"Sit!"

They dared not disobey; she was now coming towards them, birch in hand. One or two of the boys on the back row sniggered.

"Out here, Cartwright – hands!"

The unfortunate boy slowly left his seat, stood at the front and held out his hands. Jon noticed that his jacket seemed to be at least two sizes too small. Swish! The cane flew through the cold air and landed accurately across both palms three times. The boy doubled up in pain but said nothing, only staring at the teacher with hatred in his eyes.

Jon looked around the room; this was terrible, surely they were only pretending to be Victorians. A sound outside the high window made him look up. He could just make out a carriage full of people in Victorian costume riding past…

Something was very wrong about this. Jon and Rafee exchanged puzzled glances. Jon reached for the slate on his desk and scratched 'This is weird' in lead pencil, holding it so that Rafee could see.

She had eyes like a hawk.

"To me!" yelled the teacher, pointing the cane at Jon. He stood up shakily and made his way to her desk. She couldn't give him the cane, surely?

"You will both stay here after school and clean all the slates as you have defaced one with your comments…"

Just then a bell rang. Everyone stood and chanted, "Good afternoon, Miss Crabbe."

They all filed out. Jon and Rafee were left looking helplessly at one another.

"I will inspect them in the morning. Ten strokes of the rod if they are not clean!" and with that she swept out, clipping each boy across the ear as she did so.

The two friends stared after her, open-mouthed.

Somewhere in the distance a door slammed. The fog seemed to have crept into the room.

"Come on, let's go now!" whispered Rafee. They made their way quickly to the door.

They caught up with their own class eventually; it seemed that Mrs. Spencer hadn't even noticed that they had been missing. She was listening intently to the teacher in costume.

"The class would have had at least fifty children in it. The last teacher to have taught here was a certain Miss Crabbe. Apparently, she was extremely strict; she used to write down the names of the children who she had caned in this book…"

Everyone crowded round to have a look. One entry stood out to the two boys who had just arrived.

'Cartwright, for sniggering at the back of the class. Three strokes.'

Jon went rather pale.

"Mrs. Spencer," he began tentatively, "are we the only school here today?"

"Oh yes," she replied, marvelling that he had asked a

sensible question for once, "just us, Jon, and maybe the spirits of children from the past!"

Her eyes twinkled and everyone laughed... everyone except Jon and Rafee.

Chateau
de
Verre

Amber Eyes

A sleek, black cat crouched on top of the stone pillar outside the house, its amber eyes wide open in a kind of insolent stare. As the young businessman got out of the car, he nearly came face to face with the beautiful creature, who hissed at him warily. The man thought no more of it; he glanced at the paper in his hand.

'Chateau de Verre' read the address. *Castle of Glass?* he thought, referring back to his schoolboy French. A rather grand name for a strange, narrow building in the middle of a modern suburb.

The cat leaped off the pillar and strode away, stiff legged, tail in the air, turning once to gaze unblinkingly again at this intruder. It was as if the whole place belonged to this proud creature.

The high, black gates were

padlocked — so there was no easy access, in sharp comparison to next door with its open drive and neat lawn. He eventually found a small brass button which buzzed loudly when pressed.

"Who are you and what is your business?" said a distant voice.

"Er, Mr Lacey, Preferential Insurance, I have an appointment at 10.30."

No reply. Mr Lacey stood awkwardly shuffling his papers and pretending to be busily looking at them. An old lady passed by with a shopping trolley.

"Not trying to get in there, are you?" she chuckled, "they'll eat you alive!"

She laughed and crossed the road before he could question her further.

With a faint clang, the gate suddenly swung open and heaving a sigh of relief, Mr Lacey walked carefully up the loose gravel path, twisting his shirt collar rather nervously.

He knocked on the multicoloured glass panel of the front door and waited again, sweating slightly now, like a pupil waiting to see the headteacher. Why did he feel so nervous? He had made hundreds of calls like this before.

Again, mysteriously, as if by remote control, the door swung open, this time silently. He stepped inside. The same cat was sitting looking at him from the centre of a luxurious, white fur rug, as still as the Egyptian style statues that lined the entrance hall. Mr Lacey looked up, dazzled by an unexpected ray of sunlight. The ceiling was made entirely of glass. What was this place?

The whole building seemed huge inside, despite its small exterior. There were rows of glass doors leading from the hall, each reflecting the other, so that several rainbows stretched across the polished floorboards. He could smell a kind of incense, yet the atmosphere was not like that of a church, far from it. The trickle of water broke the silence and Mr Lacey turned to see a small, beautiful fountain splashing over glass crystals in one corner of the room. Then he swung round again as one of the doors opened gently.

"Please come this way," called out an anonymous voice. He followed its direction and entered a small study off the hallway. It was a tall, slim lady who had spoken. She swept her sleek, dark hair over her shoulders and held out a very pale hand, the nails sharp, almost claw-like, the beads of glass on her bracelet clinking gently together.

"How do you do? My name is…" He paused. Her light brown eyes were fixed upon him as if she knew everything about him already.

"You are Mr Lacey, and you have come to pay me the money, yes?" She smiled as she spoke, pleased at the prospect perhaps.

"Well, yes, but I need to clear up a few details first. You see, this is rather unusual…" His voice trailed off as she snatched the crisp cheque from him like an eagle snatching its prey.

"That won't be necessary; everything is in order, I will give you a receipt," she replied smoothly. Mr Lacey gulped, clutching his forms, trying to find the one that his boss had told him to get filled in at all costs. The lady sat elegantly on a red leather swivel chair and wrote on a pad with a silver fountain pen.

"There, that's all you require, isn't it?" Her voice was now almost a whisper.

"Well, actually…"

"What?" Her voice had a note of impatience in it. She turned to look at him. He hardly dared speak back; but if he didn't get this form filled in, he would get into all sorts of trouble.

He approached the clear glass table top and as he did so, he experienced a strange floating sensation in his head and everything seemed suddenly very blurred. He didn't feel at all well. If only he could get some fresh air. All he could do was focus on the colour of her eyes which seemed to be getting paler, more golden – he was swimming in a sea of gold; the colour was dragging him away.

Then all at once his whole body seemed to go limp and he was dimly aware of the sensation of fur around his face. He was being carried along; it was as if he was floating in midair. Yet he didn't panic. His brain was too muddled for that. Darkness blacked out all his thoughts for a moment and then he began to see vague shapes in front of him. He rubbed his eyes and could just make out his own car. The door was open, the keys were in the ignition and the engine was running.

He dragged himself onto the driver's seat and slammed the door shut. Not trusting himself to drive, he sat with his head on the steering wheel, his heart pounding and his hands clammy with sweat.

A thump on the car's bonnet made him lift his head. The same black cat had jumped onto his car and sat motionless, staring through the windscreen. Without another thought, Mr Lacey thrust the gear stick forward and stamped on the accelerator.

The cat was gone. The car swerved onto the road and

his mobile rang shrilly from the hands-free kit. Mr Lacey's shaky forefinger just managed to press the button.

"You forgot your receipt, Mr Lacey, do call back again." He cut off his phone; no way would he ever go back there again.

Days later, the receipt arrived on his desk with the rest of the morning post, and right in the corner was the unmistakeable shape of a paw print.

Do Something Scary

Whenever they mentioned skiing, she would get a tight knot in her stomach and pretend she didn't hear. Eleven-year-old Katie had suffered a fairly horrid accident a couple of years previously: broken her thumb, bruised her ribs and her pride. When the rest of her family had gone to France the following year, she had stayed at home with Nan. But now there was no excuse: time to put things behind her, they said, face your fears…Well, it was all very well for them, they hadn't catapulted into the air and had to be whisked down the mountain on a stretcher, much to her embarrassment.

So she agreed to go, but as soon as she said it, regretted that decision. Dad booked the flights quickly, in case she changed her mind. No going back now. Maybe she would be ill and couldn't go, maybe there would be no snow…

They got her back on skis at the local ski slope called 'The Snowdome'. She hated going and took ages to snowplough very stiffly down the first slope; but little by little her confidence grew and she managed to slide uncertainly down from the top. First obstacle over, maybe she would grow to like it after all. But every visit was a struggle and as the holiday approached she grew more and more nervous.

Everyone else in the family was simply bursting with excitement. Mum loved the scenery and the shopping.

Katie's brother Chris just adored skimming down the steepest slopes he could find and Dad imagined himself as an Olympic competitor! So Katie just went along with it all and made sure she had her new safety helmet packed away.

They arrived in Bulgaria to green slopes! Katie pretended to be disappointed but inwardly cheered. However, they were assured it would definitely snow soon and anyway, there was artificial stuff being sprayed out from the strange yellow canons onto the courses. Her heart sank and all too soon she found herself standing nervously waiting for ski school to start. The others gave her a hug and said brightly that she would be fine; then they vanished into the swirling snowflakes that had just started to fall.

The tall, totally cool instructor was very thorough and taught the group well. Katie told him about her accident and he gave her special attention to make her feel more confident.

"Rel*aa*x," he said in his strong accent, "don't worry. You will be fine!"

Well, it was all right for him; he'd probably skied since he was three. But eventually, jollied along by the rest of the group, she did gradually begin to enjoy the sessions.

At the end of the third day, when they ventured onto some real slopes: Katie learnt that the others were all going home and the old fears returned. She didn't want to go into a more difficult group.

"You'll stay with me!" said the instructor in his sing-song voice, "I'll keep a special eye on you!"

So the next day she tried her best. They put her in a group with several older children who were all at secondary school and had absolutely no fear. She was easily the worst and the others pretended not to be impatient when she was so slow on the steep bits.

The following afternoon she made up her mind to just go off on her own and not tell her parents because they would try and organise something for her. After lunch she made it look as if she was going back to her lesson, but in reality just went up and down the nursery slope which was, by now, almost obscured by freezing fog. Thoroughly wet and miserable, she took herself to the café at the bottom and ordered a welcome hot chocolate. She managed to get a chair by the roaring log fire and pretended to be busy on her mobile. Two more days to go. If only she could have stayed in the bottom group.

The next day was a lot brighter; the sun crept over the mountains creating a soft pink light and everything around her sparkled. It was stunningly beautiful. Katie made up her mind to try a blue run which led right down to the town. Her parents would have been so cross if they knew she was out of ski school; it was such a dangerous thing to do, but she just didn't think she could cope in her new group. Tentatively she set off; slowly, pretending to be confident, shuddering as everyone dashed past her. The snow boarders were the worst, skidding to a halt inches in front of her shaky skis. But gradually she began to enjoy the gentle slopes and started to appreciate the pretty woodland that lined the route.

With no warning at all, an inexperienced snowboarder smacked into the back of her; she fell sideways, lost a ski over the edge and landed face down.

"Sorry!" he called cheerily and set off again with not so much as a backward glance.

She managed to stand up, shaken, but not really hurt, and managed to retrieve her right ski. For twenty minutes she tried to get it back on again, not understanding why she couldn't cram her boot back into the tight space. On the verge of tears and dreading the phone call she would have to make to her dad if she couldn't sort it out herself, she sat down in the snow. Suddenly, a pair of skis appeared by the side of her and a small, gloved hand offered to help her up. Katie looked up and saw what appeared to be an elderly lady in a quirky, bright pink bobble hat which sat on top of her helmet.

"It looks like you could use some help, my dear," she said in a soft voice, "now let's just get you up, shall we!"

Katie staggered to her feet and the old lady expertly examined her ski.

"Oh, you need to flip it open, that's all!" She jammed her ski pole into the back lever, knocked the excess snow out of the way and helped Katie refit her boot.

"There, now, where are your parents or group?" she asked, as if she knew the answer.

"Out on our own, are we? Tut tut, too dangerous, you know!" She popped on a pair of oversized orange goggles. "Now you just follow me and I'll get you to the bottom." So they made their way with Katie following in her tracks, negotiating the steep parts slowly and carefully. Eventually, they were back at the gondola station. The old lady helped Katie into the swinging seat compartment and then jumped in herself, their respective skis safely in the carrier on the outside. As they sat and glided back up the mountain, the lady told her how she had started skiing as a young girl when it was quite frowned upon.

"We had to wear thick tweed skirts and strap our skis to our shoes!" she chuckled, "I used to be so scared, but determined to do it! After all, you should do something scary every day!"

When they reached the top, the old lady made Katie promise not to ski on her own again and with another chuckle made her way to the café.

The next day Katie let her dad and brother give her a lesson after explaining about ski school and she did start to enjoy the experience. "Do something scary every day." The old lady's words stuck in her head. She shared them with her family as they sat down to a bowl of hot soup at lunchtime.

"Well, that sounds like good advice, as long as you're careful too!" said Mum, "Oh, thank you!" The elderly waitress lifted the plates away.

"Good advice indeed!" this same waitress muttered to Katie who looked up in astonishment; it was the lady who had helped her to safety. She just smiled, said no more, but straightened her funny, pink bobble hat and took the tray away.

"What a funny old soul!" whispered Mum.

"Imagine her on a pair of skis!" laughed Chris. Then for some reason Katie looked up above the mantelpiece. On the rather grimy wall there was a faded newspaper article about the same lady, in much younger days, on a pair of wooden skis with a large medal round her neck.

Katie grinned.

"Come on," she said brightly, "let's try that blue slope again!"

Doing The Right Thing

Matthew scanned the list three or four times. There must be some mistake, he thought wildly; his name was missing! Then the truth dawned on him; he hadn't been chosen, he wasn't good enough. The crowd of his eager classmates were still struggling to see the neat print, but Matthew slunk away, embarrassed, almost tearful, with a cold, heavy feeling in his stomach. He wandered out onto the playground, not wanting to talk to anyone, burying his head inside the collar of his scruffy coat.

It had been his greatest ambition to get into the school football team, ever since Year 3. He had dreamed of standing there in assembly – "Matthew Mulligan scored a hat trick this week, a superbly skilled player" – he had seen it all; not likely now, was it? He kicked at a stray crisp packet. What's more, Dublin Unwin hadn't been to all the practices and he had been picked. Tears of indignation trickled warmly down his cold cheeks. He brushed them away furiously. He didn't care – much.

Everyone was trying to be kind; all of his best friends had been chosen, even Jacob Holland who was really a gymnast and didn't have proper boots. It just wasn't fair.

The afternoon ticked by slowly, as if to prolong the agony. He just wanted to go home to block it all out.

Geography was even more excruciatingly boring than usual, which made things worse as it gave him more time to think and feel sorry for himself.

"Never mind," whispered Jacob behind his hand, "you can come and support." Matthew didn't reply, not trusting himself to speak without crying openly.

The afternoon ended at last. The team were allowed to go five minutes early to change. Their proud, over-serious faces irritated Matthew beyond belief.

"Look at those show offs," he muttered to Ella Dulton, who was completely disinterested, flicking chewed up paper across the table and blowing bubble gum flat across her mouth when Mr Taylor's back was turned.

Matthew walked home alone and let himself in. He quickly slammed the door and, racing upstairs, flung himself on the bed.

"I'm never going to football again, ever!" Suddenly, the phone rang shrilly in the hall. He was tempted not to answer, but his mum always moaned if he didn't collect messages. He picked up the receiver unwillingly but couldn't quite believe what he heard.

"Matthew? Yes? Well, we need you to play after all – Jake is ill and so is the reserve – do you think…?" He didn't need to be asked twice. Boots retrieved from the back of the sofa where they had been flung dramatically less than five minutes ago, he was out of the door in a flash. They needed him; he would save the day…

He didn't know what made him stop, but suddenly he became aware of someone just along the pavement, someone who didn't look quite right. A frail, old man was bent right over the gate to number 84 – as if he was stuck to it. He

checked his stride and looked again. His face was drained of colour; veined, freckled hands grasping desperately at the rusty bars. He heard the church clock strike the half hour, fifteen minutes to kick off. He faltered, there was no time… Then the man dropped to the floor. He had to do something. Looking frantically about for help, he bent over him.

"Are you all right?" he asked rather feebly. He didn't answer; his eyes were closed.

Five minutes to kickoff and no one to help. A battle raged in his head: *My one chance*… The thought faded into insignificance as he realised what he needed to do. He searched the man's shopping bag and found the keys to his house; he dashed into the hallway and picked up the old-fashioned house phone. Soon he was ringing 999. He had left the door open and his eyes never strayed from the feeble form curled up on the damp floor.

The ambulance soon arrived. They all patted him on the head and said he was a good citizen and they would let him know how he… Matthew didn't hear – he'd had his chance and missed it; why did things never go right for him?

He decided to walk up to school and see how the team had got on without him. It was only then that he noticed it was raining hard: huge teardrops of rain splashing onto his tatty trainers and soaking his sports bag.

"It's all right," shouted Jacob as he rushed out of the school gates with his jacket over his head, "the match is postponed, pitch is waterlogged – good job too, where've you been…?"

Look Into The Future

Jessica liked Sundays. Her mum always took her to see her aunt; and now that she was ten, she was allowed to go off and play around the estate. They had managed to fit her new micro scooter into the boot of the car, and Jessica couldn't wait to get out.

"Wait till I've stopped the car properly and say hello to your aunt first!" said Mum firmly, knowing her daughter well.

Jessica raced up the drive and held her hand flat against the bell, making it ring non-stop, disturbing the Sunday morning peace of the avenue and gaining one or two disapproving looks from the car-washing neighbours.

She was off, as soon as the scooter could be wrenched out of the car. Off for an hour's freedom of fun and imagination.

Jessica was quite happy to play on her own. She had many friends, but sometimes preferred her own company, transforming her bike into a horse, her scooter into a jet-propelled starship chaser...

The pavement had just been resurfaced, and what's more, it sloped downwards. She managed to get to the bottom of the road holding only one handlebar. She made her way as fast as she could to the furthest part of the estate

— built in the 1950s next to an elegant, but rather dilapidated mansion house which had stood since the 1700s.

Suddenly, Jessica was aware that she had gone so fast she had arrived directly opposite this old building. The space adventure continued in her mind and she directed her chaser towards the tall iron gates.

'No Entry' stared coldly at her... she found a nice convenient gap in the bushes. Anyway, Mum said that she used to play here as a girl, so it was all right – wasn't it? A small prick of doubt stirred in the back of her mind, but there was no going back now.

She was standing on a rough path which led to a walled garden. It was a surprisingly warm autumnal day and the wind blew gently through the richly coloured leaves, rustling them like old parchments. With some difficulty she pushed her scooter along in front of her and then decided to leave it hidden in the old summer house which appeared around the corner. Jessica vaguely remembered her mum talking about the day she and her friend had found a summer house but they had been too scared to play there. Jessica smiled; she wasn't scared at all, was she? The wind had grown chillier and the sun had vanished behind a sudden crop of grey clouds. It was so quiet. The birds seemed to have stopped singing and it was somehow dark in this part of the garden.

A slight rustling noise made Jessica turn sharply. She peered into the gloomy corner where the sound had come from, just in time to see a tiny brown mouse scurry into the long grass outside the entrance. It didn't bother her; she was fond of small, furry creatures. As she looked she saw the dim outline of a large box. She touched it tentatively, her strong sense of right and wrong telling her that she shouldn't meddle. It wasn't hers, but it was interesting all the same.

As her eyes got used to the gloom, she saw that it was made of solid dark wood with strangely modern carvings on the side which reminded her of the Picasso picture she had copied at school. She ran her fingers lightly over the lid and the heavy padlock that secured it. Amazingly, it sprang open at her touch. Hardly daring to breathe, she gently lifted the lid.

Instantly, a bright light streamed out and the lid flew backwards. She looked inside and saw something so strange; it was as if this was all part of her imaginative game. It seemed as though she was looking down from a high building into a scene in the future. There were clouds floating at the top and below them all manner of fantastic aircraft, the like of which she had never seen before. Minute people stood on roads that seemed to cross in midair. Fascinated, she leaned over the edge to see more.

"Interesting, isn't it?" Jessica wheeled around, terrified. A small boy in a completely black tracksuit stood in the door frame. His face was extremely pale and his eyes a disturbingly vivid green.

"Do you want to see more?"

"Er, yes please, I think so…"

Again, the warning signals flashed before her. She was probably trespassing.

He swept his small hand over the top of the futuristic scene and it changed instantly. She could see her aunt's house and something else – smoke was coming out of the downstairs window; a blurred face was at the glass, frantically banging. What did it mean?

"What's going on? Is that happening now?" Jessica cried out loud.

The boy didn't answer, merely drew his hand across the scene and the clouds covered it all. He pushed the lid down firmly and signalled for her to go outside. She did so shakily. Then panic gripped her.

"I've got to go, just in case!" Her words were almost a whisper. The image of her aunt desperately banging on the window never left her mind as she scooted back as fast as she could up the tarmac slope to her house, her heart thumping with the effort. As soon as she got there she banged on the front door. No answer. Heaving the heavy garage doors open, she found Mum and Aunt busily weeding in the garden.

"Whatever's the matter? You look as white as a sheet!" declared her aunt, putting her arm around her shoulders, "Come on, let's get a carton of orange juice." They all trooped inside into the kitchen. The smell of scorched material met them at the door.

"Heavens! It's lucky we came in!" gasped Mum.

The tea towel had slipped from its hook and was hanging dangerously near to the gas flame which had accidently been left on.

School Camp

Mum often told us stories of her childhood to perhaps illustrate a point, and this is one of my favourites. It was about a time when she went away on her first camping holiday…

The whole of the 'Fourth Year Juniors' as they were called in the 1960s, were going away to camp and a few of the 'Third Years', who were deemed mature and sensible enough, were also invited; I was one of them. In those days, no one had any equipment and sleeping bags had to be begged or borrowed from all sorts of dubious sources. Mine was a lumpy cotton checked variety acquired from a next door neighbour who had a caravan. By the smell of it, we presumed it had been kept in the kitchen. Nevertheless, grateful for the loan, I arrived at school on a blisteringly hot day in June, everything bundled up neatly. My parents remained cheerful as we boarded the huge coach with the Welsh Dragon on the side. I didn't think twice about leaving them; I was just full of excitement.

The journey to South Wales seemed to take forever. The boys constantly asking to go to the toilet, sick bags being passed hurriedly down the aisle and green-faced unfortunates being hauled to the front seats. Eventually, we arrived at the campsite, but in those days it was just a large field with a decrepit washing block and a few spider and moth infested toilet cubicles. It cost a shilling for a bath. I decided very quickly that I wouldn't need one all week, much to my mother's dismay on my return.

We helped to set up the tents and chose our 'roommates'. There were three of us in ours – me, Helen and Janet. Helen was my absolute best friend and Janet was also one of the people who I enjoyed playing acrobatic games with in the playground. We stuffed our respective sleeping bags into the tiny tent. Nobody told us to make sure that the end of them didn't stick out of the door zip and so, consequently, when it rained they got so wet and soggy that we were unable to put our feet to the bottom all week. But we didn't care; we were adventurers, after all.

Everyone was encouraged to do jobs around the camp and Helen and I were forever cooking sausages or washing up, while Janet always had the knack of being busy when help was asked for. We didn't question this; it was just her way and we let her get on with it. Nowadays, there would have been more of a sense of injustice, but then it didn't seem to matter.

We had many adventures: walking, climbing, horse riding and even a spot of kayaking on the ancient vessels kept at a nearby lake. Health and safety was never an issue; we didn't even wear life jackets, we just had to confirm that we could swim!

Towards the end of the week we all trooped into the nearest seaside town to buy all sorts of cheap souvenirs to take home in pink, stripy bags. We crammed back onto the coach, sunburnt, giggly and very tired. Most of us had spent every last penny, but I knew I had a solid half a crown left in my pink zip-up purse. I was saving it for a wooden match holder that I'd seen, which I knew my dad would love. They sold them at the scruffy campsite shop.

Later that day we were all playing a last game of rounders at the back of the campsite while the teachers packed up, even wearier than us. It was so hot that I stripped off my hand knitted cardigan and rushed to our tent to throw it in. I could just make out Janet sitting on my sleeping bag in the gloom, with my pink purse in her hand.

"Oh, it was on the floor!" she muttered, her cheeks flushing red. Again, I didn't judge, just returned to finish my game.

At tea time I knew it was my last chance to go to the shop and I hurried to find my purse to buy the match holder. I realised straight away that the coin wasn't there. Disappointed, I searched fruitlessly. Janet helped and so did Helen. I couldn't help but think of Janet with my purse in her hand. I told no one of my suspicions, feeling hurt all the same.

It was lovely to get home. Dad was waiting as the coach pulled up, a welcome bottle of lemonade and a glass in his hand, before the days of canned drinks. I talked non-stop about the events of the week, but never mentioned the money incident as it would have spoilt the memories of an otherwise perfect holiday.

A few days later mum had just returned from the village shop. She looked a little upset and asked me to talk to her in the kitchen. I racked my brains to think what I might have done to upset her, but it wasn't me that was at fault.

"I've just seen your friend Janet," she said in a hushed voice, "goodness me, her family must be very poor, they couldn't pay their grocery bill; but then Janet found half a crown in her pocket and it was all sorted out. She must have forgotten it was there." She didn't ask me if I knew any more, but said:

"If we can help that family in any way, you must let me know…"

Then I had to tell her everything. Mum listened without comment and then said, "Well, you had no proof, but if she did take it, it seems like it was for what she thought was a good reason. So we'll leave it at that. Some people lead very difficult lives that none of us know about, and I am proud of you." She hugged me fiercely.

Shut Fast

"We are going to be so late!" moaned Rob, pacing up and down the hall, "and we've got swimming first thing!"

He rattled the door handle and kicked the bottom panel furiously.

"Oh, well, that really helps!" shouted his sister Mal. "Do something useful, can't you?"

Both parents were at work, it was five to nine and the journey to school took a good ten minutes. The front door simply would not open. They decided to try the back door, but that was notoriously difficult; even Dad struggled to turn the handle. Mum was always nagging him to do something about it. Rob grabbed the front door key from Mal and ran back to try again, twisting it with both hands.

"Now look what you've done!" Mal exclaimed, as it was obvious that the small, gold key had jammed in the lock. "We're really sunk now!"

Suddenly, they saw the outline of a figure coming up the front path.

They both banged on the frosted glass, yelling frantically, to no avail; two brown envelopes and a magazine slipped through the letter box and the postman made a hasty retreat.

"Those kids should be at school!" he muttered to himself, turning up his iPod.

Both children scowled at one other, each inwardly blaming the other for their predicament. Rob thought wildly of similar situations on TV and imagined himself smashing a chair through a window or aiming a gun at the lock. Meanwhile, Mal, the more level headed of the two, was reaching for the phone. Rob snatched it off her.

"You can't phone Mum; she's doing that presentation this morning, she'll kill us, and Dad is half way to Wales by now!"

"How about Mrs. Hammond then? She's got a key." Mal grabbed the address book and then threw it to one side. "Oh no, she's ex – directory!"

Mal took the telephone pad and proceeded to carefully write down a list of names of people who could help. Rob raised his eyes to the ceiling and muttered something along the lines of "Give me strength!" then he excitedly ran into each room to try the windows. He leaped up the stairs three at a time and then yelled back down to say that the front bedroom window was open and could they make a parachute? Mal was meanwhile ringing all the names on her list, ignoring the increasingly wild suggestions from upstairs.

Suddenly, without warning, the lights, which were still on because it was such a dull day outside, started to flicker and then went out completely. A large, grey cloud seemed to be gathering at the front of the house. Rain spattered the offending front door and a rumble of thunder could be heard in the distance.

Despite her common sense attitude, if there was one thing Mal didn't like, it was storms. She ran to the foot of the stairs, gripping the banister tightly. Rob peered down at her, his face covered with a cheap, green Halloween mask;

43

the wide mouth grinned at her in the half-light and she screamed at the top of her voice.

"Ha ha, come here, my pretty!" Rob ran down to chase her, enjoying any chance to tease his older sister.

They both stopped abruptly in the hallway. A dark, hooded shape seemed to appear behind the frosted glass of the door. They both ducked automatically and crept upstairs without a word.

Mal made it first into the bedroom. By now the storm was raging all around the house. She peered over the cold windowsill and could just make out the strange form standing below. It seemed as though this odd person was covered in rags, shiny wet as it stood in the pouring rain.

Then the thumping started.

Gently at first, a regular beat on the glass of the front door, then more erratic and increasingly heavy. It was Rob's turn to scream. Mal put a hand over his open mouth.

"Shhh! He'll know we're here!" They clung to each other, hoping desperately that the glass wouldn't break.

"How do you know it's a person?" whispered Rob, visibly shaking.

"Oh, don't be silly, what else could it be?" But she wasn't convinced herself.

Just as the noise was becoming truly deafening, the rain stopped. A thin ray of weak sunshine pierced the cloud and all was silent. They both peered out of the window. He, or it, had gone.

It was at least a quarter of an hour before they both summoned up enough courage to creep downstairs. With shaking hands, Mal tried the door once more. It swung open

easily, revealing nothing but a few autumn leaves blowing gently across the step.

Later, when they finally admitted to their parents what had happened, Mum looked at them strangely and said something quite out of character.

"You know that was your godmother's front door. We kept it when her house was finally knocked down; it was so beautiful and strong. She used to say she felt as if it was a shield, protecting her from the evils of the world."

She didn't carry on, but put her arms around their shoulders and pulled them both towards her.

Sports Star

Every Wednesday, straight after school, Fabio would dash in and get changed into his basketball kit. It was 'professional' basketball training in the local secondary school gym at 6pm; Dad had said if he did the washing up every weekend, he could go to the new club that had just started. Not that washing up was very appealing, but hanging out with children his own age, and more importantly, on a proper basketball court, was a real incentive.

For the first few weeks they went in together, as Fabio was a naturally shy boy; but once he made friends, his dad knew he would be fine. So on the fourth week, Fabio declared that he would be quite happy to make his way in from the car park on his own. It was pouring with rain, so he covered his tight, curly hair with an oversized but trendy hood, slung his kit bag over his shoulder and dashed into the changing rooms.

Straight away there was an oddness about the place. The door, which was normally constantly opening and shutting with people barging in, stood silent. Fabio, rather taken aback, pushed it open gingerly. The whole place was deserted — not one person in sight. All the lights were on and he could see the gym was also lit up through the adjoining door. He walked into that huge space and sat on a bench, a little nervous by now. This was all a bit strange. Assuming a cool attitude, he sauntered back into the changing area in case any of the others had arrived. No one. Maybe the school was shut this week? But he could hear the Irish dancing music from the room next door. Perhaps Dad was still in the car park?

Fabio ran along the wet tarmac just in time to see the tail lights of his father's car disappear out of the school gates. He had no option but to return to the silent sports block. If nobody came he would have to wait here for an hour till Dad came back.

"See, I knew I needed a mobile!" Fabio muttered to himself crossly. At ten years of age, his parents had considered him too young for this luxury, despite his protestations. All at once, he could hear a rumble of thunder overhead. The rain simply belted down and he had no option but to return to the changing room.

He considered asking the Irish dancing teacher what was going on, but that would be acutely embarrassing in front of a group of haughty-looking, leotard-clad teenage girls. So he sat again on a bench in the gym and thought vaguely about finding the basketballs and practising on his own; but all the cupboards seemed to be locked. Just as he was summoning the courage to go and find help, the stiff double door was pushed open with a creak. Fabio breathed a sigh of relief, but it wasn't one of his teammates who had opened it.

It was a boy of possibly the same age as Fabio, but he was painfully thin, with a face so pale it was almost as white as the gym wall. His clothes were extremely wet, but even so, they were obviously not sports gear; in fact, they

were almost like an odd school uniform: white and slightly luminous.

"Hello," said the strange child nervously, standing just inside the door as if he was frightened to come in. Water literally dripped from his tousled, blonde fringe onto the shiny floor.

"Have you come for the basketball?" asked Fabio just as timidly.

"What?" the boy answered in a puzzled voice.

"You know, the training, it's on a Wednesday." Fabio didn't think he knew what he was talking about. Then to his dismay, the boy burst into tears. He covered his face with his bony hands and sank down to the floor.

"I'm lost! I'm such a long way from home!" He continued to cry: great racking sobs which echoed around the empty gym.

Fabio, who was always kind and caring to everyone, put his arm around the boy's thin shoulders:

"Don't worry, I'll help. Where have you come from?"

"Metropolis Two," whispered the boy.

Fabio said he had no idea where that was, but soon chatted away to his new companion and at least succeeded in stopping his tears. They both decided they needed to get some help and Fabio fished out his old tracksuit top so that his new friend would at least be warmer.

By now the rain had stopped and Fabio, braver in the boy's company, suggested that they find the office as they both needed to contact their parents.

"What's your name?" enquired Fabio, a little cautiously.

"Zak Thirty-Four," the boy replied with a smile which displayed totally cool blue braces on his front teeth.

The office of course, almost predictably, was empty, with a 'Back in five minutes' sign at the front desk. They both sat on the faded, red leather sofa in the corridor and grinned at each other. This was quite exciting after all. Then Fabio spied an old basketball in the lost property box.

"Let's just borrow it and bring it back later," he suggested.

Zak nodded. Fabio didn't quite get the Thirty Four bit, but this boy was really, well – modern, after all. Then they raced back to the gym and tossed the ball from one side to the other. Zak didn't seem to know the rules but was a quick learner and they had quite a laugh, even scoring a few baskets along the way. For a change, Fabio felt in charge and although he didn't boss Zak about, it felt good to be able to help someone with a new skill.

Fabio slammed the ball successfully into the shuddering net; then he said that they ought to go and try the office again. So they sped across the playground, bouncing the ball between them and narrowly missing the parked cars.

Just as they came to the office door, what seemed like a huge flash of lightning lit up a massive section of the night sky. They both flung themselves to the ground and the basketball rolled away unnoticed. Suddenly, there was a deep, rumbling noise more like an aircraft than thunder and Zak stood straight up as if to attention.

"Get down!" hissed Fabio, squirming away to the side of the path. "Try to get under the bushes!"

But Zak remained standing stock still as if mesmerised by the light. Then to Fabio's horror, he began to walk towards it and eventually seemed to disappear into the whiteness. Within a few seconds, everything went black and

Fabio was left on his own, cowering under the privet hedge.

At the same time he heard shouting and saw several people running across the playground towards the gym. It was the people from his club. He ran uncertainly to join them, not sure what to say.

"Where've you been?" he asked one tall, skinny lad.

"What do you mean?" he replied, looking puzzled. "It's only just gone six!"

Fabio took part in the training session, but wasn't really concentrating. He was glad to get home. How come the whole adventure had taken no time at all? Where did Zak go? He didn't try telling his parents; it sounded, well, daft really, but continued to wonder about it all the same.

The next week, Fabio hung around making himself deliberately late, much to Dad's annoyance. He wasn't exactly frightened by the whole thing, just, well, a bit shaken; but he was relieved to see all the usual faces there when he arrived. At the end of the session, a rather harassed member of the office staff came with a shiny package under her arm.

"Have you a Fabio in this class? There's a parcel for him, as if I haven't got enough to do…" She dumped it down on a bench and rushed out.

The others all laughed and gathered round as he opened the silver paper which seemed to have a hologram effect on the outside. Out fell his old tracksuit top and a note in a silver envelope. They all groaned and started to drift off home. Lost property, how boring!

Fabio didn't open the envelope until he got back to his bedroom. There was a single slip of translucent, flimsy paper inside. It read:

Thank you, Fabio, for helping me and for lending me your clothes. It was great playing the game. I got home safely after all. Look to the south tonight. Z.

He stared out of the window just in time to see a spectacular shooting star.

The Mad Professor

The trees dripped quietly on that foggy afternoon. Big Ben could be heard: a muffled sound, rather eerie, suggesting to the imaginative that something wasn't quite right with the world. An old Edwardian house stood on the edge of the park. No passers-by even bothered to look at the dark, ornate windows. No lights shone to provide any suggestion of comfort. None at all. This was the house of Mr Timms, the strange professor. No one ever saw him in the local shops. He didn't have many callers, and when the milkman called for his money on a Friday, the door was just opened enough to enable a gnarled hand to offer crumpled notes to the poor man. He always made sure it was his quickest visit; he had no desire to stop for a chat.

The tarnished mirrors of the house reflected the pale, bony face of the professor, his eyes almost black in the dim light, glinting underneath bushy eyebrows; he would look at himself and practise his false smile which revealed his yellowing teeth.

In contrast, this strange character had a really sensible, down-to-earth housekeeper who organised all his everyday needs. She had brought along two lively children, her nephew and niece, to stay for a while as their mother was ill.

The boy's name was Joshua. He had a mischievous grin

and a good supply of freckles. The girl was called Faith. She had 'freaky' hair as she called it – bright red with masses of tight, unruly curls. They were both very fond of exploring and adventure games of all kinds.

One particular afternoon in the half term holiday, the children weren't allowed to play outside, as the fog was "bad for their chests", their aunt insisted. It drifted around every corner of the garden, reaching with its eerie fingers around the whole house.

"Come on, let's have a look at some of the rooms we haven't seen before," said Faith, cheerfully.

"Okay, but let's make sure we stay out of the way of old Yellow Teeth!" muttered Joshua. The professor would sometimes appear unexpectedly round corners and leer at them.

They both crept stealthily along the dusty passageways of that tired, old building. Before long they came to a huge door and just about managed to push it open. It was as cold as ice in the room they had entered…why did they feel so strange?

"Nothing in here!" whispered Joshua and then gasped in horror. The brown leather swivel chair in front of them swung round and Mr Timms grinned at them both, his yellow stained teeth in full view.

"Can I help you, my dears? No? Well, you are just in time to help me with my experiment!" Both children drew back, frightened. The door slammed shut as if pushed by an invisible hand and they could hear the sound of bolts being slid across the other side. No escape.

The professor, who they both, by now, privately thought was quite mad, produced a glass jar of what looked like small colourful sweets.

"Now, you just have one of these!" His slimy voice made both children shiver.

Joshua and Faith looked at each other and winked. They both took the sweets, but only pretended to eat them, and craftily slid them down the corner of one of the soft, dilapidated leather chairs which they were standing by.

Joshua wiped the stickiness left on his hands down the side of his trouser leg and nudged Faith. The professor seemed to be drifting off to sleep, waiting, it appeared, for the tablets to take effect, for that's what the sweets really were. Joshua had guessed; heaven only knows what they would have done to them.

As soon as he began to snore softly, both children backed out silently.

"Run!" Faith whispered and they both scrambled down the staircase, tripping and sliding in their haste. At that moment their aunt appeared, asking angrily why they were running.

"It's him, the professor...!" Faith was almost crying with fear.

Just then a huge crash was heard at the top of the house, followed by a chilling scream. Everyone looked up and a huge hound with a matted, grey coat appeared at the top of the stairs. It was dribbling. It looked towards them and seemed to grin, showing huge, yellow, stained teeth.

"I didn't know there was a dog here!" exclaimed Joshua.

"There isn't," his aunt replied.

The children cowered behind her; the image of those teeth remained with them for a very long time.

The Man With The Long Hair

The cold rain spattered the car windscreen as she sat in the supermarket car park. Tuesdays were always a bit dismal, and today's weather did nothing to cheer up the young girl sitting waiting for her mum to return. Ebony fiddled about with the radio controls and only succeeded in producing a confusing buzz. She idly stamped the side of her fist on the steamy window and added toes to make it look like feet. They always had to get Grandma's pension from the post office on a Tuesday, despite Ebony insisting it would be easier to get it paid into her bank account online. Mum said it wasn't just about collecting the money; it was more to do with offering Grandma some company for an hour or so. But the whole thing seemed a long drawn out process to the school girl who wanted to get home to collapse in front of the TV.

She sighed, yawned and stretched out on the front seat. Out of the corner of her eye, she saw something flapping in the considerable breeze. An elderly man in a very smart, shiny, blue suit was crossing the car park very purposefully. Nothing surprising about that, apart from his very odd hair. It was a cross between gold and grey, stretching right down to his waist, beautifully kept as if it had been blow dried and straightened.

How odd! Ebony thought casually and watched him as he crossed the main road surprisingly quickly.

At that moment, Mum came back, tired from working all day, rather damp and a bit flustered.

"I forgot the pin number!" she groaned, "how embarrassing!"

"Mum, did you see that man with the really long hair?" muttered Ebony, still looking out of the window.

Mum was too intent on getting out of the car parking space to really hear and just nodded.

When they got to Grandma's, she was a little more interested.

"Oh yes, that's Mr Crombie. Years ago, the children around here used to say he was a wizard!" Grandma chuckled.

"Really, Mother, what nonsense! I've never seen him before," yawned Mum.

"Oh, before your time, dear," continued Grandma. "They say he can still perform magic!"

Ebony forgot about him completely until the weekend. Grandma lived near a village green, overlooked by old Victorian houses and a dilapidated pub. They enjoyed taking her for a stroll there sometimes on Sundays and today Ebony had brought a new netball along. She perfected several runs and imaginary shots. As she ran ahead, she lobbed the ball a little wildly and it landed deep into the front garden of the last house.

"Oh, Ebony! You'll just have to go and ask for it back!" Mum always liked to do things right. Ebony squirmed uncomfortably; she hated talking to strangers.

"Can't I just go and fetch it?"

"No, go and ask!"

The reluctant girl walked slowly up the unkempt path and lifted the tarnished knocker which was too stiff to make much of a sound. Eventually, the door scraped across the floor as if it was sticking. To her amazement, there stood the man with the long hair she had seen in the week. He had on the same smart, blue suit and his hair was just as perfectly styled.

"How can I help you...?" he asked in a gentle, surprisingly young sounding voice.

"Um, I'm sorry, my ball..." Ebony was quite pink with embarrassment by now.

"Oh, no problem!" The man smiled to reveal perfectly white teeth.

Then the offending ball seemed to gain a life of its own and bounced towards her. As she picked it up and was about to rush off, Mum called out to her:

"Ebony! Quick, Grandma's not well!"

Grandma had collapsed on the path and was making strange noises. Ebony was terrified and tried to find her mobile. Without hesitation, the man with the long hair seemed to glide to the end of the path and knelt down beside the crumpled form. Mum was crying and desperately trying to get a signal on her phone.

"Don't worry," said the man in smooth, even tones, "she'll be fine."

He passed his smooth hands over Grandma's forehead and all at once her eyes flickered open and she smiled.

"Mr Crombie, how nice to see you!"

The doctor at the hospital couldn't quite understand it. Grandma had suffered a kind of fit and should have been unconscious. He scratched his head.

"You must have had your guardian angel looking after you, Mrs. Coleman!" he smiled. "Off you go, you're fine!"

A few weeks later they went to see Mr Crombie to thank him, but there was no answer, even after several attempts with the stiff knocker.

"Oh well, we'll send him a card," said Mum, noting the address.

Ebony shuddered slightly as the wind blew a few white feathers across the garden path.

The Var

A small child of about three with long, auburn ringlets and a very pale face, stood in her back garden one cold February morning. She was an only child, but never seemed to miss having brothers and sisters, as even at this early age she had a vivid imagination and invented characters to keep herself amused.

The grass was soft and muddy and she was playing an absorbing game with old sticks and pebbles, much to her mother's annoyance as she kept wiping her sticky fingers down her old-fashioned duffle coat. The world was a fascinating place and she was happy to play, talking to herself in hushed tones.

A sharp wind blew her sticks down and she lifted her soft blue eyes towards the sky as if in mild annoyance at having her game interrupted. As she did so, she saw a dark shadow appear at the tiny window of the old cottage at the bottom of the garden on the other side of the sturdy privet hedge. Emily, for that was her name, was easily frightened and rushed into the kitchen to grab her mum's legs.

"Hey, what's the matter, Em?" her mother asked patiently, used to this sort of panic in her young daughter.

"Shadows in the window…" Emily muttered, a fresh tear running down her cold cheek.

"Now, now, Em, that's not shadows, that's a vase of lovely flowers on the windowsill," soothed Mum almost automatically and returned to the washing.

Not convinced, Emily went back outside, but stayed near the comforting bricks of her own house, furtively looking up at the tiny window. But the ominous shadow didn't reappear.

From that day Emily made up a story in her own head about the lady who lived in the house. She was called 'The Var' as she had misheard her mum's explanation. The name stuck and the rest of the family referred to 'The Var's house' as if she were a real person. No one was really sure who lived there; no one was ever seen in the small space behind the hedge.

Occasionally, as she grew older, Emily asked about 'The Var', and Mum would weave believable stories about how she was a very kind lady, and indeed, would throw lollipops over the fence if the little girl next door was very good…

Around seven years later, Emily's ringlets had been trimmed and stored in a creased envelope for sentimental reasons. She remained a happy-go-lucky character, full of fun and energy, on the brink of going to secondary school. A lover of all sports, dancing and acrobatics, although there was little money to pay for proper clubs, Emily practised in her garden, sometimes with friends, but still quite as happily on her own. One evening she was just perfecting a daring balance at the top of her old swing and as she hung upside down she caught a glimpse of a shadow behind the hedge. All her old fears came back to her, although she told herself not to be so silly. After all, it was probably just 'The Var'!

She did a somersault and jumped down, looking warily

through the hedge, not really wanting to see what was there. The hedge rustled in the fading light. Was it a person, an animal, or just her imagination?

Emily didn't mention it to anyone; her Dad would have made a huge joke about it all. But as she made her way up to bed that night, she decided to have one more look out of her bedroom window. Since she was ten she had moved to the bigger room which overlooked the back garden and you could see right across to the strange little cottage at the end of it.

"Night, night!" she called down, trying to sound quite normal, although for some reason as the daylight slipped away she felt a little anxious about the whole thing.

She took a long time getting into her night clothes, almost putting off looking out at the dark back garden. Eventually, she screwed up enough courage to peer over the windowsill. Maybe she wouldn't see anything anyway. It was all a bit daft really. She didn't convince herself though.

As her eyes grew accustomed to the dark, she could just make out the privet bush moving slightly. Well, it was a windy night...Then suddenly she saw it clearly. A small, bundled shape stepped out from it onto the lawn. It was unmistakeably a little old lady who seemed to be pointing her walking stick straight up in the air. After she had got over her initial shock, Emily pressed her nose against the glass in an effort to see what she was pointing at. The small figure stepped forward and shakily pointed again towards the roof of the house; then she turned and the hedge seemed to swallow her up.

Emily's curiosity overcame her fear and she called downstairs, "Mum, Dad, there's something on the roof!"

She sprinted downstairs and ushered her bewildered parents out of the back door. They all looked up into the night sky and, to their amazement, saw the TV aerial hanging precariously by one single cable.

The emergency team that arrived to make it safe, said it could have fallen at any moment and caused considerable damage. Emily was praised for her powers of observation. She later told her parents everything; they looked at each other with raised eyebrows, but the next morning went round to the front of the old cottage to see if they could thank the old lady who had warned them.

The young woman who answered the door was really pleasant and helpful, but said there was no old lady living there now; they had bought the house ten years ago from her family. Apparently, when she was alive, she had been a really kind soul, always helping others, a really good neighbour...

Trapped!

"If you don't get a move on, it will be dark and we'll never find our way home!"

Spencer's voice sounded slightly panicky as his two friends struggled to keep up with his long strides. The grass was getting wetter and wetter, almost a jungle on this side of the country park. Everything seemed wilder here and there was a deep silence all around, except for the tramping of their feet, soaking wet by now.

"Just slow down, will you!" gasped Isaac, "I bet you don't even know if we're going the right way!"

"Well, have you got any better ideas, Chewitt?" Nadia spluttered. Isaac had been given this name through constantly munching on gum, sweets or even bits of paper when times were hard. Nadia pushed Isaac on to avoid tripping over his huge feet.

The watery sun had disappeared altogether and menacing clouds were gathering ahead of them. The day had started well enough – a trip out on their own at last.

"We can trust you now you're in Year 6 – can't we?" Spencer's parents had agreed and after much phoning round had cleared the idea with everyone else. So they had all gone exploring with their lunch, a compass and Isaac's mobile phone – just in case.

'Survivor' had sounded like a really good game to play, but it involved visiting parts of the country park where none of them had ever been before and consequently, they were all hopelessly lost.

"That's it; I just can't go on!" Isaac proclaimed dramatically, "energy resources are nil!"

"Someone put a sweet in his mouth, for goodness' sake!" muttered Spencer irritably. It had been his idea to come this far and he didn't like to admit that he didn't know how to get home.

Isaac flung himself on the grass and rolled about, mouthing "Food, food!" rather pathetically.

Suddenly, a dark object fluttered across their path like a Halloween bat, making them all duck instinctively. It turned out to be a kestrel chasing its prey, oblivious to the children. Nadia screamed as she saw it grappling with a furry object, blood oozing from its claws. Spencer signalled for her to be quiet and rushed over to see more.

"Ugh, it's disgusting!"

Nadia covered her face and backed away. The boys were poking at the unfortunate mouse with sticks, the kestrel having dropped his catch after seeing the children. Isaac's snapped and his hand closed on a cold metal handle almost hidden in the undergrowth.

"Nadia, come here!" the boys shouted at once.

"No fear!" Nadia remained where she was, but peered through the gloom.

Isaac pulled at the handle but only succeeded in coating his hands with rust; the boys then all pulled together to no avail. Nadia edged forward.

"Well, try twisting it," she said, practical as always. As

they did as she suggested, a kind of stone lid lifted up with a sharp creak, mud and roots dangling beneath it.

"If you think I'm going down there…" her voice trailed off, unnoticed by the boys who were already starting to climb into the space below.

"Oh, come on, don't be such a wimp!" Isaac taunted, knowing she would follow.

He produced his pocket torch with a flourish and lit up

the earthy passageway that led steeply downwards from the surface. Nadia gingerly followed, being careful not to touch the sides in case a spider or other unmentionable creature fell into her long, thick hair.

"Wow, look at this!" Isaac's voice seemed a long way in front of them; the others held onto each other, blinking into the dusty torch beam.

They saw a large bird cage, covered with dust. It must have been there for ages.

CRASH! A heavy thud echoed above them.

"The trap door!" Isaac ran back along the dark tunnel, only to confirm their worse fears. Someone or something had slammed the stone back down over the entrance.

"Good job I have my phone!" Isaac said smugly, whipping it out from his pocket. It beeped feebly – 'battery low' flashed momentarily across the tiny screen.

"Oh, great!" Spencer snatched it from him, panicking again. It was totally useless. Nadia suggested they switch off the torch to save the battery on that.

No one said anything. The darkness seemed to close around them like a heavy cloak. Isaac got up and started to feel for the cage. Where was it? He switched on the torch. Nothing, only disturbed earth where it had stood.

Nadia screamed again. Spencer covered his ears but then put a comforting hand on her shoulder.

"There must be an easy explanation," Isaac whispered quietly, "there has to be!"

He felt all around the walls and suddenly his fingers rested on two screws directly in front of him. He pushed them tentatively and the whole wall gave way. A mouth of a hole showed up in the torchlight.

"Come on, it's a way out!" yelled Isaac, diving head first into the passageway ahead like a rabbit.

The others followed. The tunnel seemed to close in on them as if trying to squeeze them in its dark grasp. Then, oh joy! Light – just a pinprick far ahead. No one said anything, but pushed on, desperate to get to the fresh air.

They tumbled out beneath a large oak tree silhouetted against the evening sky.

"Look!" cried Nadia. The same kestrel, it seemed, was again whirling overhead, looking at them sideways.

"Do you think it shut you in then?" A man's voice came from behind them. The bearded ranger wasn't smiling but there was a twinkle in his eye.

"Nice evening for a walk," he said, "plenty of wildlife about…"

Whispers From The Past

It was a beautiful spring day. The bright, fresh sunshine made even the dullest objects come to life. The frost lay thick on the grass and it sparkled as if waking from its winter sleep. Jack sat in the back seat of the car with his nose pressed against the glass. A weekend away with his family was a daunting prospect, but it was such a gorgeous morning even he could not be downhearted for long.

Dad had managed to get a really good deal: a four star hotel complete with swimming pool, bike hire and more importantly, a fabulous skate park, which meant putting up with Nan and his annoying younger sister was a small price to pay. It was going to be a great start to half term.

After a hugely boring trip to the retail park en route to the hotel, everyone tumbled out of the car and Jack raced ahead to check out the directions for all the attractions.

"Jack, slow down, for goodness' sake!" sighed Mum, but smiled all the same. It was good to see him so excited. He was rather an odd child, even she could see that, preferring his own company or that of his many pets to children his own age – just the opposite to his sister, Charlotte, who had a different friend for every day of the week.

The extremely efficient receptionist booked them all in and Mum went off with nan to settle her in.

"We're in the stable block," grinned Dad, "hay for breakfast then!" The family room was huge and Jack claimed the single bed next to the window. He drew the curtain as it seemed to be quite cold despite the large old-fashioned radiator underneath the windowsill. They left the unpacking and went straight down to dinner. Jack, of course, was starving and ate his four courses with relish.

"Can we try the skate park out, Dad?" asked Jack eagerly as soon as his meal was finished.

"Sorry, son, it closes at five!" grinned dad, "but we'll go first thing in the morning, that's a promise.

"I don't want to go!" sulked Charlotte petulantly.

"Don't worry, you and I will go swimming," soothed Mum, "let's go to the games room and play table tennis!" She would have secretly preferred a nice, long soak in the freestanding bath, but she always put herself last.

Nan did a good job of umpiring the game and then insisted on telling them the history of the hotel.

"It used to be a coaching inn, back in the eighteenth century," she began, her eyes sparkling. She loved old stories. "It was owned by a large family. I think there would have been lots of children running around the place!"

"Just like now," laughed Dad, "I bet you can still hear them having fun!"

"What do you mean, Dad?" Jack was immediately scared; he hated the idea of anything supernatural.

Mum shot him a look.

"Dad's being daft!" Mum said lightly, "don't take any notice."

But Jack thought about it all the rest of the evening and didn't look forward to going to bed. Charlotte, however, was very excited and jumped from one bed to another.

"Can we leave the light on?" whispered Jack to his mum as she tucked him in.

"I'll leave the lamp on by your bed," she said reassuringly, "don't take any notice of Dad's teasing!"

He lay there for a long time without sleeping, listening to every creak and rustle. His sister snored; she didn't care about... ghosts? He shuddered under the crisp, white duvet and covered his head so that he couldn't breathe. His mum and dad had stopped whispering in the king size bed at the other end of the huge room. It was so cold in here; he covered his head up once more.

Then he heard it clearly. A child's voice, a whisper:

"What's the matter?"

Jack froze.

"Don't be scared!" continued the voice, "just find my box. It'll be in the garden."

Then nothing. He must have slept eventually and in the bright light of day, he felt rather foolish about his fears. He confided in Mum after breakfast.

"Just a dream, Jack," she squeezed him tightly. She had been as sensitive as him in her younger days, and yes, the room did feel cold...

He suggested to Charlotte that they could play in the walled garden at the back of the stable block. He didn't consciously choose to do this; it just came into his head.

"Well, all right, but I'm not playing rugby again, you're too rough!" She stuck her tongue out. They both laughed. Charlotte was all right really.

So they played a kind of cross between basketball and

netball and then after a particularly wild shot towards the battered ring which was fixed to the fence, the faded, orange ball disappeared in the undergrowth. Jack raced after it and slid feet first under a thorn bush which promptly tore the threads in his new sweatshirt.

"Ha ha! Mum will go mad!" Charlotte giggled.

Jack's feet dug deep into the topsoil and as he pulled the offending ball towards him, he could feel something solid stopping him slipping any further. He dug into the dirt with his hands and uncovered a battered box with a heavy padlock securing it. The words he had heard the night

before came flooding back:

"Just find my box…"

"What on earth are you doing?" hissed his sister, anxious to get on with the game.

Jack showed her his curious discovery, but she was unimpressed.

"Ugh, it's got cobwebs on it; throw it in the bin, it's probably just junk!"

So Jack appeared outwardly nonchalant and yet when Charlotte had gone to get a drink from the café, he took the box to Nan. She always seemed to know what to do.

"Well, it does really belong to the hotel as it's in the grounds. Let's find someone in charge." Nan couldn't contain her excitement. "Who knows what might be in it?"

As luck would have it, the owner of the hotel was on duty at the desk that afternoon and when Jack presented it to her with nan looking on from behind him, she was open-mouthed.

"Oh, my goodness, I wonder…?"

"What?" stuttered Jack.

The elderly, silver-haired lady put her hand to her neck and on a fine silver chain was a tiny key.

"If this is the box I think it is, then all my worries are over!"

With trembling fingers, she fitted the key into the padlock and after a moment or two they all heard a satisfying click as the padlock fell open. They all peered inside.

A light brown, faded piece of parchment lay folded at the bottom of its patched, blue velvet interior. The owner picked it up carefully and spread it out in front of her. They crowded round, nan fumbling for her glasses.

"Well, I never!" sighed the lady. "My family have been

looking for this for so many years! It proves that the house is mine and can never be sold out of the family. The hotel chain wanted to buy it instead of renting it from me. I nearly gave in. But this is my great great grandfather's will, which says it cannot be sold!" She burst into tears.

Horrified, Jack ran to his Nan.

"Jack, don't worry; it's tears of happiness! How did you find it?"

Later that evening, Jack again told Mum all the details including how he knew where to find the box. She just hugged him and didn't try to say it was all his imagination.

As he lay in bed he noticed that the atmosphere in the room was much warmer. He no longer felt frightened and just as he was drifting off to sleep he wasn't even surprised to hear:

"Thank you."

About the Author

Melody Starkey has been a primary school teacher for thirty-five years, working around Birmingham and Coventry. She has taught all subjects, but for the past seven years has been an Advanced Skills teacher for Dance and P.E., and continues to work in that area in schools around Coventry as a consultant.

These stories have evolved from material that she devised for her own lessons in school and to entertain her pupils; some of whom gave her the ideas for these characters and events.

She is keen to ensure that creativity in all its forms is on offer for all children, and maybe these short adventures may inspire more writing, music, dance or art.